The Day The Chocolate Melted Away

By Uncle Dave Howard

Illustrated by Maria DeSimone Prascak

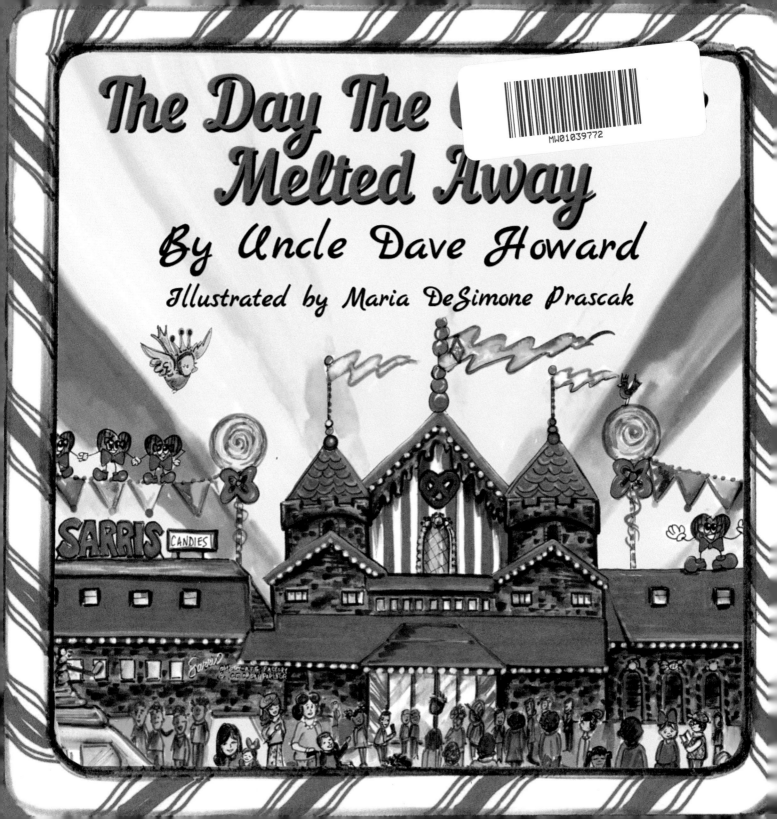

www.sarriscandies.com

www.mariasideas.com

Other books by Uncle Dave Howard

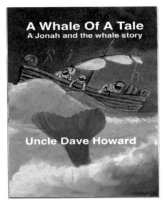

And many more!

www.uncledavesbooks.com

www.uncledavesbooks.com

Thank you!

The store was founded by a man named Frank. He is the one we all have to thank, for the best little candy store all around. Down in Candiesburg, a very sweet town.

Frank Sarris 1931-2010

Far away in Candiesburg, a very sweet town, was a candy store named Sarris. It was the best around. They had ice cream and candy bars. They had jelly beans and toy cars.

They had Marshmallow Peeps and lollipops, candy that's sour and sweet, and gum drops. There were gummy shaped fish that were every kid's wish.

They had giant stuffed toys for girls and boys. They had a player piano that played itself, and chocolate candy that filled every shelf.

The chocolate castle was big as can be that all the kids wanted to see.

The store was founded by a man named Frank.

He is the one we all have to thank

for the best little candy store all around,

down in Candiesburg, a very sweet town.

Then one day a fire broke out.

"FIRE! FIRE!" someone did shout!

"Hurry! We must call 911.

There is a fire! Please hurry! Please come!"

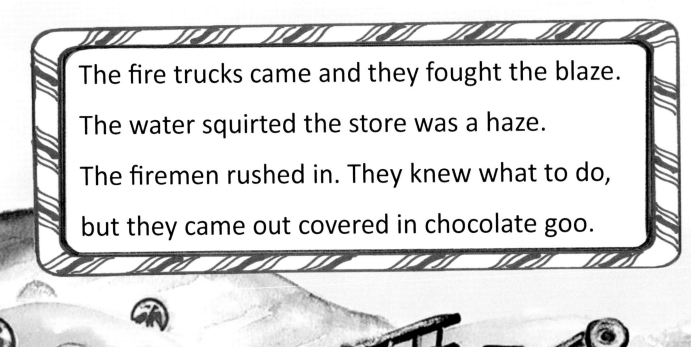

The fire trucks came and they fought the blaze.

The water squirted the store was a haze.

The firemen rushed in. They knew what to do,

but they came out covered in chocolate goo.

Now the fire was out.

People did shout, "Oh no! All the chocolate! The toys! What about the girls and boys?"

Then the owner, whose name was Bill, stood tall and said, "Be Still! We will rebuild! We'll clean this up A.S.A.P. You just watch me!"

Then some people cried, some people sighed, some said it couldn't be done, and some said it's not going to be fun.

Then a little girl with chocolate brown hair

said her name was Anna Clair.

She stepped out

and started to shout,

"Never say never!

We can make it better than ever!

If we work together as one

We might just have some fun!"

Then the whole town pitched in and cleaned off the shelves. They were all busy like Santa's little elves. The piano is all right and so are the toys! Anna Clair was jumping for joy!

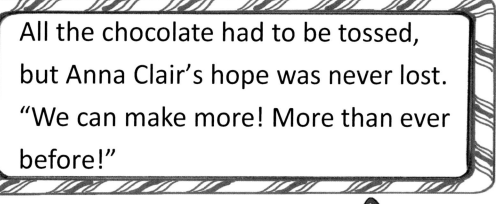

All the chocolate had to be tossed,
but Anna Clair's hope was never lost.
"We can make more! More than ever
before!"

"Let's turn on the machine and get it going. Let's get our famous chocolate flowing!" They quickly made chocolate candy bars and restocked the shelves with candy and toy cars.

When they reopened the store the whole town was at the door. They bought the candy and the toys for all their little girls and boys. They were all happy to be in the store. It was better than before.

Thanks to Bill who was willing to rebuild at any cost, even after all he lost, it was again the best candy store around, down in Candiesburg, a very sweet town.

Maria DeSimone Prascak is a self- taught artist best known for her custom murals and fine art in her home town of Pittsburgh, PA. Her art is described as enchanting, colorful, imaginative and aesthetically pleasing. Painting professionally since 1982, she's had the opportunity to apply a variety of mediums such as acrylic, watercolor, pen and ink, airbrushing and mixed media. Influenced by her client's requests, the subject matter varies from landscapes, imaginary, architectural to wildlife, nature and pets motivating her to learn different techniques, for example, realistic, trompe loeil, impressionistic, imaginary, expressionistic, whimsical, and old world styles.

Over 450 feet of Maria's murals can be seen throughout Sarris Candies in Canonsburg, PA., and multiple areas of The Pittsburgh Zoo & PPG Aquarium, numerous local restaurants cafes, homes and businesses.

Maria's art is sold online, at local art shows, sole exhibits, and the gift shops at the National Aviary. She was the featured artist for the Aviary's Wings & Wildlife Art Show 2017.

Featured on local tv, radio and a variety of publications, her art is current, often influenced by her life. She is active in local communities "giving back", aiming to inspire others through her work and teaching classes. Passionate about art since childhood as she wrote and illustrated her own books and created art, she was determined to become a full-time artist. Maria is immersed in art and works closely with her client's, bringing their ideas to life.

For more info: **www.MariasIdeas.com**

Uncle Dave Howard Is an award winning children's book author and illustrator. He has won U.S.A. best books, International best books, Mom's Choice Award and Five Star Readers Favorite. He has a BFA from California University Of Pennsylvania . He was born with dyslexia, ADD, and Asperger's. He visits schools and libraries giving motivational and anti-bullying speeches. He has authored over fifteen books to date. He lives in Murrysville with his wife Ruth. Check out his books at

www.uncledavesbooks.com

Pipe Cleaner Pretzel!

Supplies needed: Brown and black Chenille stems and sew on or glue on eyes. We used sew on here.

(1) Twist one brown stem like the picture and you can just twist the extra around itself

(2) Cut the black stem into 2 long and 3 short so you have 5 black pieces

(3) Use one of the short and twist around center of pretzel and you can insert the stem into the holes of the sew on eyes or glue them onto the black stem.

(4) Twist on two long for legs and two short for arms

and you are done!

Made in the USA
Middletown, DE
14 January 2020